# SUPPANDI & FRIENDS

*Tinkle* mash-up stories have always been at the top of the most-requested list from readers. There's something about seeing Suppandi, Kalia the Crow, Tantri the Mantri, Shikari Shambu and other *Tinkle* Toons in the same story. For the first time ever, we present to you a collection filled with only *Tinkle* mash-up stories!

These include special stories from *Tinkle*'s classic 100th and 200th issues. There's also a special story from Billy Drain the fangless vampire of the comic horror series Dental Diaries, teaming up with Aisha from SuperWeirdos— and so much more!

Plus! Suppandi laugh-out-loud adventures pepper the pages!

The combination of so many *Tinkle* Toons really made this issue bloom. I love seeing my favourite characters together.
**Srilekha M., Rajahmundry,** *Andhra Pradesh*

It's a good idea to bring our favourite Toons together. That way we get double the entertainment in a single story!
**Shivansh A.S.**

I love *Tinkle* mash-up stories. I eagerly await more such mash-ups.
**Tapasya Marathe,** *Mumbai*

# MARCH OF THE TINKLE BRIGADE

Script: *Dev Nadkarni* and *Iyer Prasad B.*

Illustrations: *V.B. Halbe*

4

...AA...

TICHOO!

WHAT HIT ME?

HEH HEH! I DON'T KNOW. YOU WERE OUT COLD AND. WE HELPED YOU COME TO. HEH HEH!

I SAY, YOU LOOK FAMILIAR. HAVEN'T WE MET BEFORE?

AH, YES...

WE'VE MET IN **TINKLE**.

YOU'RE CHAMATAKA AND HE'S DOOB DOOB.

...AND YOU'RE TANTRI!

THANKS FOR THE GOOD TURN YOU DID ME. NOW WHAT CAN I DO FOR YOU?

OURS IS A TALE OF WOE...

...AND ALL BECAUSE OF ONE FEATHERED FOE.

WHO'S THAT?

KALIA THE CROW.

CAN YOU HELP US GET RID OF HIM?

AND A SINISTER PLOT IS HATCHED—

REST ASSURED. I'LL FINISH HIM OFF FOR YOU.

EXCELLENT!

HEY, THERE'S KALIA HAVING A DRINK...WRING HIS NECK, FRIEND.

THAT SHOULDN'T TAKE LONG.

JUST THEN—

?

SWISH SWISH

7

···AND SOMEWHERE IN THE PROCESSION—

KEECHU I'M HUNGRY.

DON'T FRET. THERE'S SOME DELICIOUS GRASS UNDER THOSE COCONUT TREES.

HEH HEH. THOSE FOOLISH RABBITS.

I DON'T LIKE THE WAY CHAMATAKA'S EYEING US.

HEH HEH, I RECKON I'LL GET THOSE RABBITS NOW.

COME HERE, LITTLE RABBITS.

GO AWAY. GO AWAY.

MEANWHILE—

AH! THE GREAT SHIKARI SHAMBU. I'VE HEARD A GREAT DEAL ABOUT YOUR EXPLOITS. I'VE ALSO HEARD THAT YOU'RE A CRACK SHOT.

HEH HEH, SO I AM.

···BUT I DON'T BELIEVE IT.

WHAT?

GOOD SHOT! BUT DON'T BE SCARED OF THE TIGER. HE'S ALSO COMING WITH US.

I TAKE IT ALL BACK, SHAMBU. YOU'RE INDEED A CRACK SHOT.

AND SO—

BUT—

SO MANY RABBITS.

CHAMATAKA ALWAYS TAKES ME FOR A FOOL. BUT I'LL SHOW HIM.

I'LL GO AHEAD AND HIDE IN SOME BUSH AND GRAB ME A RABBIT OR TWO.

12

13

SOB SOB

HEY, BOY. WHAT'S THE MATTER? COME, TELL ME ALL ABOUT IT AND I'LL HELP YOU.

SUPPANDI TELLS ALL—

WHY, THE ANSWER'S SIMPLE.

JUST CHANGE HANDS. TRANSFER THE GROUNDNUTS FROM YOUR LEFT HAND TO THE RIGHT...

...AND THE DAL FROM THE RIGHT HAND TO YOUR LEFT AND THERE YOU ARE.

CLAP! CLAP!

BRAVO, HODJA. JUST WHAT WE EXPECTED OF YOU.

AND NOW WE MOVE ON.

14

...AND AFTER MANY HOURS OF TREKKING...

...AND FLYING...

...THEY ARRIVE IN BOMBAY.

WHEN —

WHERE'S MY GUN? MY GUN... IT'S GONE!

HOW CAN I FACE THE WORLD WITHOUT MY GUN?

I DON'T HAVE IT.

WHERE COULD IT HAVE GONE?

IT'S NOT WITH ME.

NOR ME.

NOR ME.

IT WAS ON YOUR SHOULDER.

WHERE COULD IT GO?

HEY, SUPPANDI, WHAT ARE YOU DOING?

IT'S NOT HERE.

WHAT'S NOT HERE?

THE GUN!

HA HA!

HAR HAR!

HEE HEE!

HEY, LOOK. LOOK WHO'S THERE.

IT'S RANJHA AND HIS MASTER...

...AND ANWAR...

...AND RAGHU!

HEY, SHAMBU, WHY SO GLUM?

I...I'VE LOST MY GUN...

IS THAT ALL?

RANJHA, TRACK!

SNIFF!

MEANWHILE, SOMEWHERE IN THE PROCESSION—

HEH HEH! I'LL GET HOOJA FOR SURE THIS TIME

16

# SUPPANDI
## X-Ray

Story & Script:
Dolly Pahlajani

Pencils & Inks:
Archana Amberkar

Colours:
Umesh Sarode

Letters:
Pranay Bendre

SUPPANDI! THE NEW X-RAY MACHINE I HAD ORDERED HAS JUST ARRIVED. I WANT TO TEST IT... COME ALONG!

OKAY, SIR.

IN THE X-RAY ROOM—

PRETEND YOU'RE THE PATIENT. LIE DOWN HERE.

I'VE PLACED THE PLATE UNDER YOUR LEG. LIE STILL NOW...

HEY! WHERE ARE YOU GOING, DOC?

BEHIND THAT DOOR. I'LL TAKE THE X-RAY FROM THERE SO THAT THE RADIATION DOESN'T GET TO ME. EXPOSURE TO X-RAYS IS HARMFUL, YOU KNOW...

# Put on Your Party Hat!

**Story & Script**
Dolly Pahlajani

**Art**
Abhijeet Kini

**Letters**
Prasad Sawant

CRACK!

THIS SEEMS LIKE THE RIGHT ADDRESS. ALTHOUGH I DON'T GET WHY ANYONE WOULD LEAVE THE DOOR OPEN.

LET'S GO IN TO FIND OUT, AGENT PARTY ANIMAL.

AS YOU SAY, AGENT GREEDY GUEST.

OI!

YIEEKS!

ARE YOU TWO DEFECTIVE DODOS SNEAKING IN? THIS IS AN INVITATION-ONLY PARTY.

HEY! WE'VE GOT THE INVITATIONS TOO, AISHA.

THAT LOOKS IDENTICAL TO MINE.

*Dear Star of Tinkle,*
*Your presence is requested on November 14 at the Casa Evala for an evening gala. Please enter before 8 p.m. so that you don't miss the main event that will change your life forever.*
*Yours in anticipation,*
*Your Host*

SO YOU SEE, WEIRDO, WE WERE JUST SNEAKING IN TO INVESTIGATE THE MYSTERY STRANGER BEHIND THESE INVITATIONS.

HMM... WE'VE BEEN TRYING TO FIGURE THAT OUT TOO.

WE? WHO'S 'WE'?

21

24

25

OOMPH!

THIS IS MY PARTY! AND NO ONE IS GOING TO SPOIL MY MAKEOVER PLANS.

NOW, FOR YOU, I WANT A DASHING, MODERN COSTUME.

POOF!

WHAT'S THIS?! I DIDN'T ASK FOR A HAT FOR YOU! LOSE THE HAT!

POOF!

HOW? I'VE ALWAYS WANTED TO SEE SHAMBU'S EYES AND NOW THESE STUPID HATS ARE DEPRIVING ME! CHANGE COSTUME!

POOF!

POOF!

NO! MY MAGIC IS FAILING ME! WHY?!

LOSS OF FAITH IN OWN MAGIC. YOU ARE GETTING A TICKET FOR THAT. COURTESY THE SOUL-SEARCHER'S MAGIC FAITH REVIVAL COMMITTEE.

FINE

NO-NO! I DON'T NEED REVIVAL OF MY FAITH IN MY OWN MAGIC! I AM LORTAI, THE MOST FASHIONABLE FAIRY IN THE WORLD! YOU CAN'T—

26

—CONFISCATE MY WAND.

READY TO GO, MADAM? BEFORE YOUR MAGIC STARTS WEARING OFF LIKE YOUR FAITH?

SNAP!

! MY PRETTY KEOVERS! GONE! OOOOOO!

POOF!

WOAH!

BOINK!

WELL, GOOD RIDDANCE, I SAY. SUCH A REPULSIVE FAIRY. IT ALMOST MAKES ME NOT WANT TO BELIEVE IN FAIRIES ANYMORE.

WELL, I KIND OF MISS MY MANE.

AND I MY FANGS.

OH, BOOHOO! TOO BAD. NOW, CAN WE GET AROUND TO SOLVING HOW HER MAGIC DIDN'T WORK ON SHAMBU?

I KNOW! MAYBE HE HAS A MAGIC REPELLENT SPRAY.

NO! A SHIELD THAT DISPELS SPELLS!

UH... TO BE HONEST, I HAD NOTHING. BUT THESE MANNEQUINS DID. AND WHEN THE SMOKE OF HER MAGIC ENVELOPED ME, I JUST GRABBED A HAT FROM ONE OF THESE HELPFUL SOULS*. I FEEL UNDRESSED WITHOUT ONE.

I SAW HIM. PITY I DIDN'T SQUEAL. SHE WOULD HAVE REWARDED ME.

WELL, WE CAN STILL REWARD YOU...

REALLY?

YES! WITH A PARTY HAT!

OW!

HAHAHA! JUST THE WAY I LIKE IT. LET THE PARTY BEGIN!

PARTY

AND I COVERED UP MY CLUMSY DARTING WITH AWESOME OSES. I THINK I'D MAKE A GREAT MODEL."

YOU HEARD THE MAN! GO PARTYYYY!

27

# SUPPANDI
## *Doctor, Doctor, Go Away!*

**Story**
T.S. Karthik

**Script**
Shruti Dave

**Pencils & Inks**
Archana Amberkar

**Colourist**
Umesh Sarode

**Letters**
Prasad Sawant

UFF! WHO IS RINGING THE DOORBELL SO HARD?

TING TONG TING TONG TING TONG

SUPPANDI! WHAT'S WRONG? WHY ARE YOU OUT OF BREATH AND KILLING MY DOORBELL?

(HUFF-PUFF) MAD— MADDY! QUICK, TELL ME...

WHAT? WHAT IS IT, SUPPANDI?

IS IT TRUE THAT AN APPLE KEEPS A DOCTOR AWAY?

WHAT?! UH... YEAH, IT IS. WHY?

THEN, QUICK! GET ME AN APPLE RIGHT NOW!

BUT WHY?!

YOU SEE, I WAS PLAYING CRICKET AND I HIT A SIXER...

...THE BALL BROKE OUR NEIGHBOUR, DR. DIXIT'S WINDOW, AND NOW THE ANGRY DOCTOR'S AFTER ME!

THAP

GREAT! WE'LL MEET YOU THERE. WE'LL CATCH THESE FOLKS RED-HANDED AND RESCUE THE INSECTS.

ER...

*CLICK*

AHA! SHAMBU DOESN'T KNOW THAT THE SNOOP & SPY ARE MOPES AND PURR UNDERCOVER!

THERE REALLY IS NO SUCH THING AS A FREE HOLIDAY.

THE PLAN WORKED! WE HAVE THE TIME AND PLACE, SAKI.

LET'S RESCUE MY COUSIN, HAMATO, FROM THE FIGHT THEN, PURR.

DON'T WORRY, WE WILL. THERE'S NO LANGUAGE BARRIER WITH SHAMBU IN OUR TEAM. NOTHING CAN STOP US NOW!

—EVENING—

WHERE ARE ALL THOSE SNOOP & SPY PEOPLE? THEIR PHONE LINE IS ALSO DEAD!

湖畔

Miyazaki

(GULP) HERE I AM. I HOPE I GET OUT OF THIS IN ONE PIECE.

PASSWORD?

THERE'S A PASSWORD? I—I DON'T KNOW IT...

HE'S HERE!

NO PASSWORD. NO ENTRY.

PHEW! THAT'S GREAT.

CAN I HAVE A PIECE OF YOUR CHOCOLATE?

NOW WHAT?

RELAX. WE'VE BEEN SITTING HERE ALL EVEN WE KNOW THE PASSWO

YAMATOSHI!

HUH?!

TAKE ENTRY. NOT MY CHOCOLATE.

(SIGH)

HE'S IN!

WE'D BETTER FIND A WAY IN AS WELL.

GULP. AND I'LL BE GOING OUT.

WELCOME TO THE JUNGLE FIGHT CLUB.

YOU CAN KEEP YOUR PET HERE. WHEN YOUR NUMBER IS CALLED, IT'LL BE BROUGHT IN FOR THE FIGHT.

33

35

Measure your height using a ruler or a measuring scale.
And remember: 1' (foot) = 12" (inches); 1" = 2.54 cm

# SUPPANDI Plant Protection

**Story & Script**
Dolly Pahlajani

**Pencils & Inks**
Archana Amberkar

**Colours & Letters**
Pranay Bendre

TODAY, JUNE 5, IS WORLD ENVIRONMENT DAY. LET US ALL TAKE A VOW TO PROTECT OUR TREES AND PLANTS. IN RETURN, THEY WILL PROTECT US.

SUPPANDI!

YES, MA'AM.

I'D LIKE YOU TO MEET MR. NARAYAN H HE'S THE MOST FAMOUS SHRUB SHAPE TOWN. I WANT HIM TO WORK ON OU GARDEN. TAKE HIM THERE PLEASE.

RIGHT AWAY, MA'AM.

A HALF HOUR LATER—

HOW'S IT GOING—OH!

SNIP!

YOU SHALL NOT PASS!

STOP! WHAT'S GOING ON HERE?!

YOUR HELPER, HE'S LOCO. HE'S NOT LETTING ME SHAPE YOUR SHRUBS!

BUT, MA'AM, IT'S WORLD ENVIRONMENT DAY.

I HAVE TO PROTECT OUR PLANTS.

WHY, YOU! WASTING MY PRECIOUS TIME! GRRRR! PROTECT YOURSELF NOW!

I DON'T NEED TO! THE PLANTS WILL PROTECT ME!

SWAT!

OW!

SEE! THEY DID! NOW IT'S MY TURN AGAIN!

I'M TOO OLD FOR THIS. ≥SOB!≤

40

# SUPPANDI ROAD RULES

| Story & Script | Pencils & Inks | Colours | Letters |
|---|---|---|---|
| Shruti Dave | Archana Amberkar | Umesh Sarode | Prasad Sawant |

# Mopes & Purr feat.
## Shikari Shambu in TRAINED DOGS

| Story & Script | Pencils & Inks | Colours | Letters |
|---|---|---|---|
| Neel Debdutt Paul | Savio Mascarenhas | Akshay Khadilkar | Prasad Sawant |

AT THE SEMINAR FOR URBAN ANIMAL STUDIES...

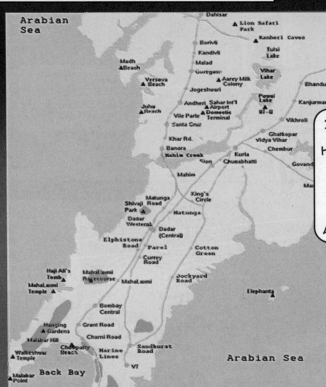

IF IT WEREN'T FOR MY FRIENDS, I WOULD HAVE MISSED IT TOO. I AM VERY GRATEFUL FOR THEM. AND I AM VERY GRATEFUL TO YOU FOR GIVING ME THE OPPURTUNITY TO ADDRESS YOU TODAY.

A FEW MONTHS AGO, I FOUND A WEBSITE WHICH CHRONICLED DOGS ON THE **MOSCOW METRO RAILWAYS.** RESEARCHERS, BLOGGERS AND COMMUTTERS HAD NOTICED A PATTERN AMONGST THEM.

DOGS HAD DISCOVERED THAT FOOD WAS AVAILABLE AT THE CITY CENTRE DURING THE DAY, AND THERE WERE ABUNDANT SUPPLIES IN THE SUBURBS AT NIGHT. THEY HAD MASTERED THE METRO SYSTEM, LEARNED HOW TO FOLLOW TRAFFIC LIGHTS, FIGURED OUT HOW MUCH TIME IT TAKES BETWEEN STATIONS, AND LEARNED TO COUNT BETWEEN THEM. THEY WOULD TRAVEL, JUST LIKE THE MASSES OF THEIR FELLOW HUMAN CITIZENS ACROSS THE CITY, FOR A BETTER MEAL.

AND THEN I DISCOVERED THAT YOU DIDN'T HAVE TO TRAVEL ALL THE WAY TO MOTHER RUSSIA TO OBSERVE THIS.

43

A FEW MOMENTS LATER...

IT STARTED A FEW MONTHS AGO. IN FACT, IT WAS BATE THAT SHOWED US THE WAY.

BATE?

WE HAD BEEN LIVING IN BANDRA FOR THE LAST 14 YEARS. AND ONE EVENING IT STRUCK ME.

PLEASE USE ME

THE HUMANS GO TO THE CITY DURING THE DAY, AND COME BACK TO THE SUBURBS AT NIGHT. IF WE FOLLOWED THEM, CAN YOU IMAGINE THE AMOUNT OF FOOD WE WOULD GET?

SOUNDS LIKE A GREAT IDEA.

SO SONALI AND I STARTED FOLLOWING THEM. WE REALIZED THAT'S WHAT THOSE TRAIN THINGYS ARE FOR. THEY GO FROM ONE PLACE TO ANOTHER.

WE STUDIED THE TIMINGS OF THE PEOPLE. WE LEARNT HOW TO STAY AWAY FROM THE BOXES IN WHICH ALL THE GOOD SMELLING PEOPLE WENT. FIRST CLASS KICKING THEY GAVE US. BUT WE FOUND A DIFFERENT BOX EVERY DAY.

I WANT TO SEE THIS.

SURE. COME WITH US.

47

48

SUDDENLY...

GAH! ITS THOSE DRATTED DOGS AGAIN!

I'D LIKE TO REPORT DOGS ON THE TRAIN AGAIN... WE ARE BETWEEN BANDRA AND KHAR. COME SOON.

HEY! YOU THERE! GREEN MAN. WHY ARE YOU FEEDING THEM? THEY'RE DISGUSTING STREET DOGS. AND CAT.

LET THEM BE.

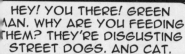

OH, I'M GOING TO LET THEM BE ALL RIGHT. LET THEM BE IN CAGES FOR THE REST OF THEIR MISERABLE LIVES.

WATCH OUT!

RUN!

49

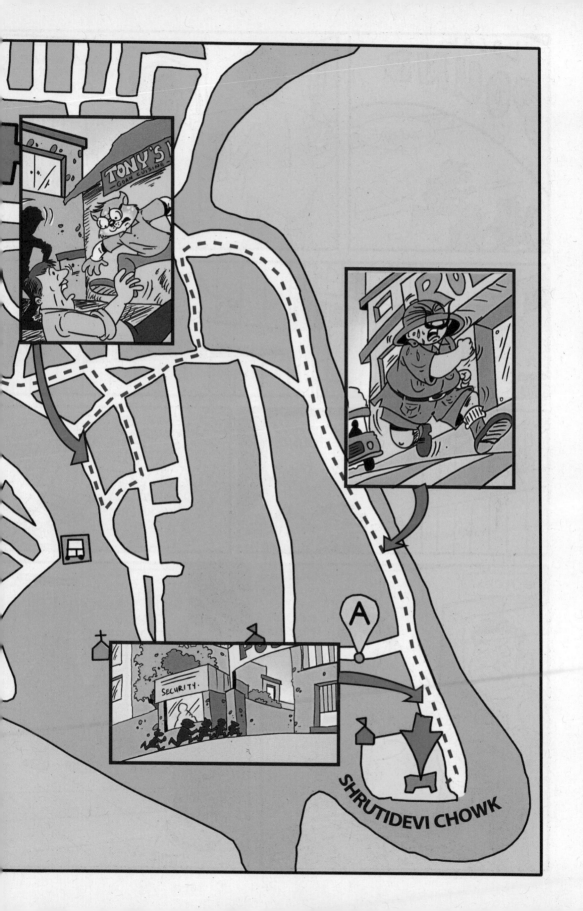

# STRANGER SIGHTINGS

**Story & Script**
Sean D'mello

**Pencils & Inks**
Vineet Nair

**Colours**
Umesh Sarode

**Letters**
Pranay Bendre

GREAT! WE'RE ALL HERE. WE NEED TO HUNT FOR THIS STRANGE CREATURE THAT HAS AIZWA SPOOKED.

I HAVE A KINGDOM TO CONQUER, PEOPLE! I DON'T HAVE TIME FOR SILLY NONSENSE!

WILL YOU QUIT DOING THAT, TANTRI?!

DUSHTA'S LATEST SMOKE GRENADES MAKING YOU NERVOUS, SHAMBU?

GUYS, QUIT KIDDING AROUND! WINGSTAR'S RIGHT! EVEN I'VE READ THE REPORTS. WONDER IF IT'S SOME SUPERWEIRDO?

I SHOULD HAVE BROUGHT MOMMY ALONG!

FINE! LET'S DO THIS THEN. I NEED TO GET BACK TO MY PLANS IN HUJLI. HERE'S WHAT WE'LL DO... BUZZ... BUZZ...

WHY ARE YOU FALLING BACK, SHAMBU? ARE YOU SCARED TOO?

ME? YOU'RE THE LILY-LIVERED FANGLESS VAMPIRE, BILLY DRAIN! I JUST DON'T FEEL LIKE SHARING MY SNACKS!

≡HMPH≡ YOU—

THUMP

55

HUH? WHERE DID BILLY GO—

ZOOP

ZOOP

JUST THEN...

GUYS! SHAMBU? BILLY?! WHERE DID THEY GO?

AISHA, LOOK! THERE'S A TRAIL OF PEANUTS. WASN'T SHAMBU EATING THEM?

THE TRAIL LEADS TOWARDS THE RELEK FOREST! LET'S GO.

AMAZING! FIRST, I WASTE TIME ON SUPERSTITIOUS NONSENSE. NOW I GET TO BABYSIT A GROWN MAN AND AN OVERGROWN BABY!

SOMETIME LATER...

THE TRAIL ENDS NEAR THE DOOR OF THAT HOUSE.

PLEASE HELP ME. PLEASE!

HELP ME!

HUH?

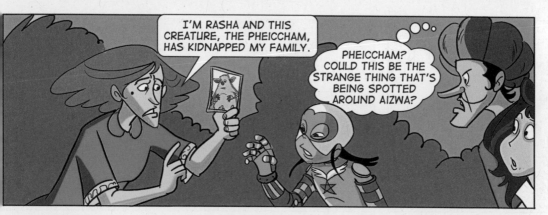

57

MINUTES LATER...

GOTCHA!

THERE!

LET'S GO! WE HAVE NO TIME TO LOSE!

=GASP=

THE POOR BABIES! THEY ARE ALL TIED TOGETHER. WHO WOULD DO THIS?

WHY, THAT WOULD BE ME!

RASHA! BUT... DIDN'T THE PHEICCHAM KIDNAP YOUR FAMILY?

HA! AND YOU BOUGHT MY STORY! I NOW HAVE ALL THE PHEICCHAMS AND THE TINKLE TOONS UNDER MY THUMB!

YOU GUYS ALSO LED ME TO THE LAST PHEICCHAM. SOMETHING I WAS HOPING YOUR FRIENDS SHAMBU AND BILLY HERE WOULD DO! THAT'S WHY WE KNOCKED THEM OUT.

SHAMBU! BILLY!

TIE THEM ALL UP! THE PHEICCHAMS WILL GRANT EVERY LAST ONE OF MY WISHES. FIRS AIZWA, THEN MIZORAM, THEN INDIA, AND THE THE WORLD. ALL UNDER MY FEET! MUHAHA!

58

62

# Say cheese'!

**Story & Script**
Sean D'mello

**Art**
Sahil Upalekar

**Letters**
Prasad Sawant

HUH? WHERE AM I? HOW DID I GET HERE?

AAAAH!

SOMEONE HELP MEEE!

AAAAH!

NO WAY! SHIKARI SHAMBU, RIGHT IN FRONT OF MY EYES!

THUD

I NEED TO FOLLOW HIM. WHERE THERE'S SHAMBU, THERE'S ALWAYS ADVENTURE!

PHWEEE

THUMP

MINUTES LATER—

YOU OKAY, KID?

UMM, YEAH, I THINK SO. MY HEAD JUST RINGS A BIT. WHAT HAPPENED?

YOU SAVED MY LIFE! THAT'S WHAT HAPPENED.

I DID THAT?

YOU SURE DID. WHEN YOU BANGED INTO THE TREE IT KNOCKED A COCONUT STRAIGHT ON TO THE LEOPARD.

HA! YOU DON'T SAY, MR. SHAMBU!

WAIT A MINUTE. YOU KNOW MY NAME?

OF COURSE I DO. YOU'RE THE FAMOUS SHIKARI SHAMBU, THE GREATEST THERE EVER WAS!

A GIANT LADDOO! YUM YUM!

PLEASE, PLEASE, DO CONTINUE.

I'VE BEEN READING ABOUT YOU SINCE I WAS—

NOOO, RAJA HOOJA! IT'S A TRAP!

HEY! WHY DID YOU DO THAT?

THUD!

JUST WATCH WHAT HAPPENS, YOUR HIGHNESS!

BOOM

THAT LADDOO WAS SET TO EXPLODE AS SOON AS YOU TOOK A BITE OF IT.

OH MY! HOW DID YOU KNOW THAT, LITTLE GIRL?

OH WELL, LET'S JUST SAY THAT I'VE SEEN THIS SORT OF STUNT BEFORE.

TANTRI, MY DEAR TANTRI! COME MEET THIS GIRL WHO JUST SAVED MY LIFE.

Rustle Rustle

⸘HMPH⸘ I SAW, YOUR HIGHNESS. YOU WERE LUCKY SHE WAS AROUND.

IT'S TANTRI THE MANTRI, IN THE FLESH! YOU KNOW, YOU'RE TALLER IN PERSON.

WHAT DO YOU MEAN BY "IN PERSON"? HOW DO YOU KNOW ME?

OH, NEVER MIND. IT'S QUITE A LONG STORY!

WHATEVER THAT *TINKLE* WRITES ABOUT ME IS ALL HOGWASH!

I'M HUNGRY, TANTRI.

YOUR HIGHNESS, I HAVE A BANANA.

⸘HMPH⸘ YOU'D THINK SHE WOULD HAVE OFFERED ME SOMETHING TO EAT TOO!

THANK YOU, LITTLE GIRL.

SUPPANDI, GIVE ME THE CAP FOR THE CAMERA, PLEASE.

SUPPANDI!

HUH? I'M BACK?! WHAT JUST HAPPENED?

ARE YOU DONE DAYDREAMING? WE'RE ALL AWAITING OUR TURN!

SOMETIME LATER...

DID THAT CAMERA FLASH REALLY TRANSPORT ME TO THE PAGES OF *TINKLE*?

HEY, WHAT IS THIS?

THANKS again for getting me out of a SPOT — s.s.

SO IT WASN'T JUST A DREAM!

I LOVE THAT SHIKARI SHAMBU HAT! WHERE DID YOU GET IT, VASUDHARAJE?

SIT DOWN, PRIYA. I HAVE THE MOST AMAZING STORY TO TELL YOU.

OKAY. BUT FIRST, DO YOU HAVE ANYTHING TO EAT?

I DID, BUT I GAVE IT TO RAJA HOOJA! HE WAS STARVING.

DID YOU JUST SAY RAJA HOOJA?

I TOLD YOU IT WAS AN AMAZING TALE. NOW LISTEN...

THE END

67

SHAMBU DECIDED TO TACKLE THE PROBLEM AT ITS SOURCE—

NOW, COULD YOU ALL EXPLAIN TO ME EXACTLY WHAT'S BEEN GOING ON WITH THE GOATS?

GONE! ALL GONE!

THEY COME AT NIGHT!

WORK OF A SNOW LEOPARD!

NOT A LEOARD, THE YETI!

WITH FANGS LIKE KNIVES!

ALL RIGHT, THANK YOU. BUT YETIS ARE NOT REAL. THE SNOW LEOPARD, HOWEVER, I SHALL SEE TO.

AND I PRAY THAT THE SNOW LEOPARD IS JUST AS IMAGINARY!

AND SO SHAMBU'S GETAWAY TURNED INTO A WORKING VACATION—

(GASP) (HUFF)

WHY DON'T I EVER LEARN MY LESSON AND JUST KEEP MUM?!

HOURS LATER—

UH-OH, IT'S GETTING DARK. MUTTON OR NO MUTTON, THE HOTEL SOUNDS LIKE A GOOD IDEA.

=SNIFF SNIFF= I SMELL HUMAN...

GRRR

RAAARRRR

AAAH!

MEANWHILE, MOPES AND PURR WERE CONDUCTING THEIR INVESTIGATION—
THESE GUYS WILL TELL YOU WHAT'S BEEN HAPPENING AROUND HERE.

OOH! I CAN'T WATCH!

BUT THEN—

YEOWWW!

THAT'S RIGHT! DON'T YOU EVER COME BACK!

JOB WELL DONE, SHAMBU OLD CHAP! HE-HE-HE!

ANOTHER PROBLEM SOLVED! AND NOW I'M OFF!

LOOKS LIKE WE'VE FOILED YOUR PLANS AGAIN, DABOO.

THIS TIME WITH LITTLE HELP FRO THE FAMOUS SHIKARI SHAMBL

PHOOEY! IF THAT LEOPARD HADN'T BEEN SCARED OFF, I WOULD HAVE BEEN FREE!

AND WHAT, OR WHO, EXACTLY SCARED THE SNOW LEOPARD OFF? OUR HEROES WILL NEVER KNOW THE TRUTH...

SSSHHH!

BUT WE WILL!

# ATTACK FROM OUTER SPACE

Script : Prasad Iyer

Illustrations : V.B. Halbe

DEEP IN SPACE AN ALIEN CRAFT MAKES ITS WAY TOWARDS OUR PLANET.

PLANET EARTH APPROACHING, YOUR MAJESTY.

GOOD. PREPARE TO HOVER OVER THE SURFACE AND CAPTURE SOME SPECIMENS FOR EXAMINATION.

WE MUST KNOW WHAT SORT OF CREATURES INHABIT THIS WORLD BEFORE WE SET OUT TO CONQUER IT.

IT WILL BE DONE, MIGHTY KING BLINKOR.

WE ARE HOVERING 500 METRES ABOVE THE SURFACE.

GOOD. NOW LOOK FOR CREATURES WE CAN CATCH WITH OUR ENERGY RAY.

MEANWHILE IN TINKLELAND, HOME OF OUR FRIENDS —

HEY, KALIA!

WHY, HELLO, KEECHU.

KEECHU, YOU'VE BECOME VERY PALE. DON'T BE AFRAID. CHAMATAKA ISN'T AROUND...

HELP, KALIA!

75

HE-HE'S DISAPPEARED! WHAT'S HAPPENING!

SQUAWK! SQUAWK!

A CHICKEN! WHAT'S A CHICKEN DOING HERE?

IT'S NO CHICKEN. IT'S JUST SUPPANDI.

SUPPANDI, YOU IDIOT! WHAT ARE YOU SQUAWKING LIKE A CHICKEN FOR?

I HAVE A PROBLEM, KALIA.

MY BOSS IS ALWAYS TELLING ME TO SAVE MONEY. TODAY HE SENT ME TO BUY A FEW CHICKENS.

GO ON!

BUT I GOT A BRILLIANT IDEA. "SUPPANDI", I SAID TO MYSELF, "WHY DON'T YOU BUY A FEW EGGS AND HATCH THEM YOURSELF? THAT WILL REALLY SAVE MONEY AND PLEASE THE BOSS TOO."

AND THAT'S WHY YOU WERE SQUAWKING LIKE A HEN, BECAUSE THE EGGS WOULDN'T HATCH!

HOW DID YOU GUESS?

NEVER MIND.

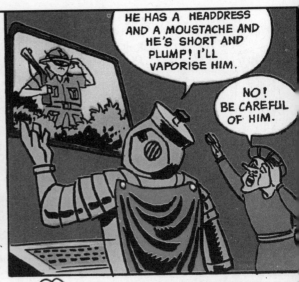

IT'S RANJHA AND HIS MASTER!

RANJHA! TRACK! SCENT!

COME ON, HOOJA! COME ALONG WITH US. WE'VE GOT TO SAVE OUR FRIENDS.

CLANG

CLANG

THERE'S THE SPACESHIP! LOOKS LIKE THEY'RE CARRYING OUT REPAIRS.

I'VE BEEN WATCHING THEM FOR SOME TIME NOW. MY DART MUST HAVE HIT SOME VITAL PART AND THAT MIGHT HAVE BROUGHT IT DOWN.

HEY! THERE'S HODJA!

HODJA! THOSE ALIENS HAVE CAPTURED KEECHU AND SUPPANDI.

MAYBE EVEN TANTRI, CHAMATAKA AND DOOB DOOB.

WE MUST SAVE THEM BEFORE THE SPACESHIP LEAVES EARTH.

RELAX! THEY AREN'T GOING ANYWHERE.

WHAT DO YOU MEAN?

I SPOTTED THE VALVE ON THE FUEL TANK AND LET ALL THE FUEL OUT. SO THEY ARE TRAPPED.

BRAVO, HODJA!

85

# 'WERE' DO YOU GO?

**Story & Script**
Dolly Pahlajani

**Art**
Abhijeet Kini Studios

**Letters**
Pranay Bendre

TING-TONG!

COMING! HANG ON A MINUTE!

BILLY! WHAT ARE YOU DOING HERE?

OH, I WAS IN THE AREA... THOUGHT I'D DROP BY. MAY I COME IN?

SURE, COME IN.

THANKS, AISHA.

I WANT YOU TO BE MY TRACKER. I'M LOOKING FOR THIS BLOKE NAMED KOUTA MARGICK WHO TURNS INTO A WEREWOLF. HE LIVES IN THE WOODS BEHIND YOUR HOUSE.

WHAT DO YOU WANT?

OH! OH NO! I INVITED YOU IN! I FORGOT—

—THAT I'M A VAMPIRE. KIND OF YOU. NOW I CAN COME AND GO AS I PLEASE, UNLESS...

I'M A SUPERWEIRDO TRACKER, **NOT** A SUPERNATURAL TRACKER. EVEN A FANGLESS DIMWIT LIKE YOU SHOULD KNOW THAT!

HEY-HEY-HEY! NO NAME-CALLING! ESPECIALLY WHEN SOMEONE HAS COMPLETE ACCESS TO YOUR HOUSE.

GRRRR...!

AS I WAS SAYING... THIS WEREWOLF CHAP LIVES IN THE WOODS, LIKE A HERMIT, BECAUSE HE DOESN'T WANT TO BE A THREAT TO HUMANS. BLAH-BLAH-SAINTLINESS.

...PROTECTING YOURSELF FIRST?

SCREEEEECH!

AAAAAARGH!

NEED A HAND THERE, *DAMSEL?*

NO THANKS. HUH.

IF YOU BOTH ARE DONE BICKERING, CAN WE MOVE? IT'S GETTING DARK AND I HAVE HOMEWORK TO DO WHEN I RETURN.

SO, HEER AND I WENT INTO THE WOODS THIS MORNING.

IT TOOK US SOME TIME TO FIND YOUR GUY. BUT FIND HIM WE DID.

A HALF HOUR'S TREK AND—

HAH! NO BIG DEAL FOR MY VAMPIRE VISION.

THERE'S THE TREE ON WHICH HIS HOUSE IS BUILT. IT'S WELL CAMOUFLAGED.

YET IT WAS NOT YOUR VAMPIRE VISION THAT LOCATED KOUTA AND HIS HIDEOUT. IT WAS ALL AISHA'S POWERS.

—VERY GOOD HEARING, YES?

ULP!

AND HEER'S IDEA OF MARKING THE TRAIL LEADING TO HIS HOME.

ALL RIGHT–ALL RIGHT! KEEP IT DOWN, WILL YOU? WEREWOLVES HAVE—

89

OUR SENSE OF SMELL IS ALSO EXCEPTIONAL. AND ONE OF YOU SMELLS—

SNIFF-SNIFF

—DEAD.

HI?

VAMPIRE. NOT OFTEN SEEN IN THESE PARTS. WHAT DO YOU WANT HERE, PARASITE?

UH... WHAT'S WITH THE HOSTILITY?

PARASITES LIKE YOU DESERVE IT! AND THE TRAGEDY IS THAT I'M LIKE YOU. I CAN BITE PEOPLE AND TURN THEM... DESTROY THEIR LIVES. JUST LIKE MINE WAS DESTROYED.

AND WHAT WAS **MY** CRIME?! THAT MY CAR BROKE DOWN IN THE WOODS, AND THE ONLY HELP AROUND TURNED OUT TO BE A WEREWOLF!

AAAAAA

AND NOW I HAVE TO LIVE AWAY FROM CIVILIZATION, AFRAID TO INFECT SOME INNOCENT PERSON. DO YOU HAVE ANY IDEA HOW BAD THE CELL PHONE RECEPTION IS IN THE FOREST?!

91

93

*"IF ONLY HE KNEW" IN HARE-SPEAK.

# SUPPANDI
## ELEMENTARY

**Story & Script**
Sana Khan

**Pencils & Inks**
Archana Amberkar

**Colours**
Pragati Agrawal

**Letters**
Pranay Bendre

SUPPANDI IS WORKING AS AN ASSISTANT TO A DETECTIVE—

AND REMEMBER... YOU'RE WORKING IN A TOP SECRET ORGANIZATION!

OF COURSE, SIR! IN FACT, I'M SO PROUD I GOT THIS JOB...

...THAT I TOLD EVERYONE IN MY BUILDING ABOUT IT!

SHEESH! SUPPANDIIII! WHEN I SAY SOMETHING IS 'TOP SECRET', ABSOLUTELY **NO ONE** MUST KNOW ABOUT IT. IS THAT UNDERSTOOD?

BUT... BUT, SIR...

NO 'BUTS'! NOW OFF TO WORK!

THAT EVENING—

SUPPANDI, TODAY'S OPERATION IS CRUCIAL.

OPERATION? IS HE A DETECTIVE OR A DOCTOR?

WE ARE GOING UNDERCOVER NOW.

BUT, SIR, ISN'T IT TOO EARLY TO GO UNDER COVER?

I GET UNDER COVERS WHEN I GO TO BED AT NIGHT.

SUPPANDI! THIS IS NO TIME TO CRACK JOKES! WE NEED TO CRACK THIS CASE!

BUT... BUT... SIR... IF WE CRACK THIS BRIEFCASE, WHERE WILL YOU PUT YOUR FILES?